D0515984

To my grandfather,
and the Soca culture
—N.B.

For Grandma Betty
—J.O.

LOVE, Lah Lah

WRITTEN BY
NAILAH BLACKMAN

ILLUSTRATED BY
JADE ORLANDO

Alfred A. Knopf
New York

Wake up, Wake up

The sun is strong, and Carnival is waiting.

Papa, Papa

Take my hand—
it's time for celebrating!

Mas bands sway 'n' dance down festive streets.

Like rolling waves, we flow with the soca beat.

Come on, Come on

High on your shoulders,
I watch the King and Queen.

Eat up, Eat up

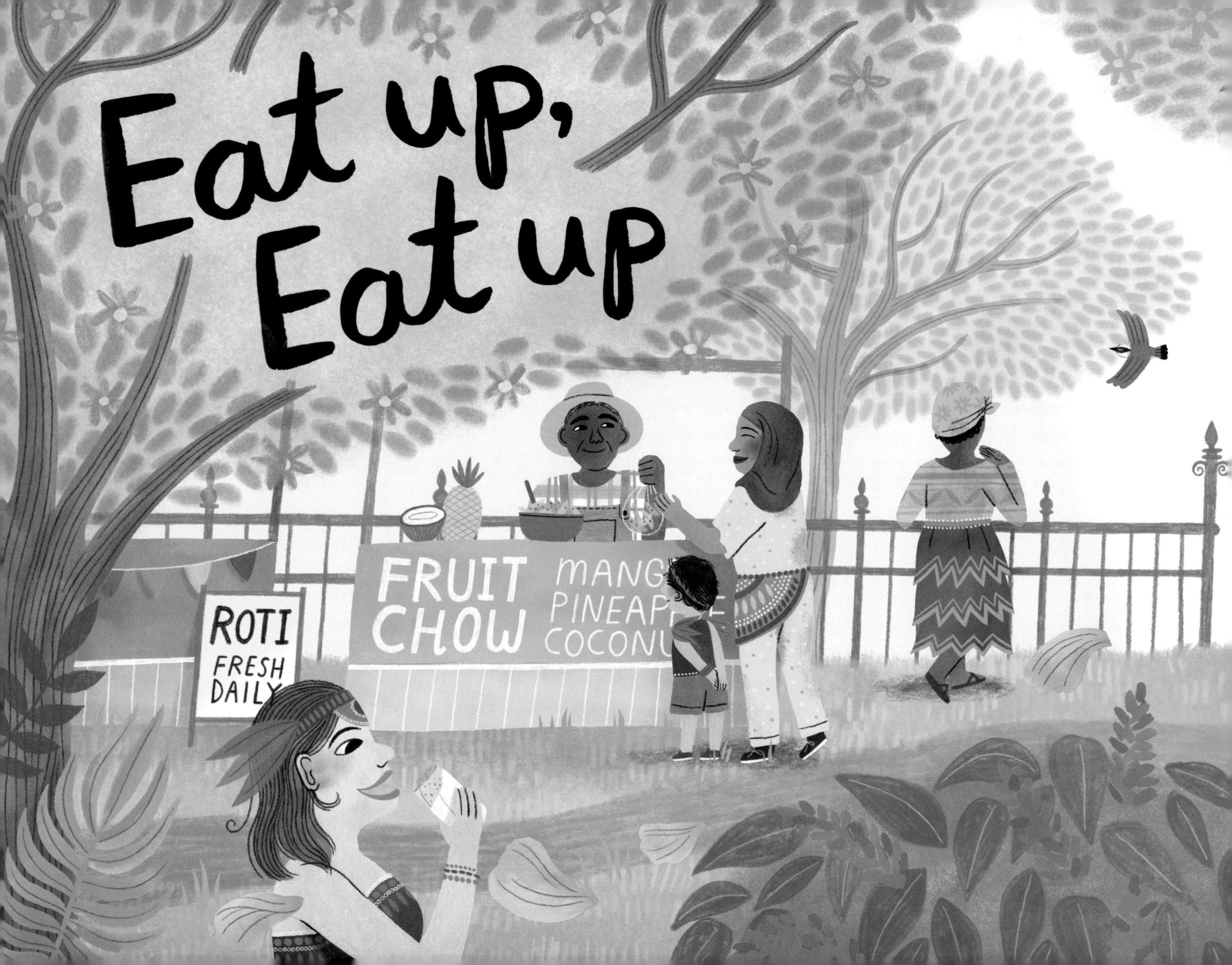

We feast on mango chow before we sing.

I hear your song. Your music calls to me.

Leh-la,
Leh-la

We take the stage.

The crowd is going loca.

Oh-eh, Oh-eh

We jammin', vibin', banging to the soca.

So very proud to be a part of you.

You're proud to be a part of me, too.

Glossary

Carnival is an exuberant celebration held every year in Trinidad and Tobago and many other countries around the world, featuring colorful costumes, parades, and cultural events. It takes place on the Monday and Tuesday before Ash Wednesday.

The Kings and Queens Costume Competition is a contest to determine the best costume of Carnival. Costumes can weigh between forty and two hundred pounds and are often enhanced with lights, fireworks, sound effects, and more!

Mas is short for "masquerade" and refers to the costumes worn by Carnival participants. Celebrants dance through the streets in elaborate, colorful costumes that capture the vibrant and joyful island culture.

Mas bands are parade-goers who march together wearing a group costume.

Soca is a popular Trinidadian style of music derived from calypso in the early 1970s, featuring fast tempos and dynamic rhythmic energy. Soca is the heartbeat and soundtrack of Carnival.

Poui (POO-ee) trees are known for their trumpet-shaped bright pink or yellow flowers and are a common sight in Trinidad and Tobago.

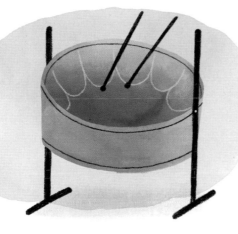

TOBAGO

PORT OF SPAIN

TRINIDAD

Steelpans are musical instruments, like drums, originating in Trinidad and Tobago. They are a staple of Carnival music!

Trinidad and Tobago is a two-island nation in the Caribbean, off the coast of Venezuela. Trinidad's capital, Port of Spain, hosts Carnival.

Ras Shorty I

Ras Shorty I is the father of soca music and Nailah Blackman's grandfather. One of his most important works was the 1974 album *Endless Vibrations*, which was the first to use the new soca rhythm.

Dear Grandpa,

Your time on earth with me was short, but your wisdom and vision will be passed on for generations to come. You taught me to be patriotic, to understand and love my culture—and for that, I am proud. Without you, we would have no Carnival as we know it, because soca music invokes the art that is Carnival. Soca mesmerizes people in the streets to walk for miles and miles without even recognizing it. And it also inspires costume designers to create the beauty that people travel from all over the world to see. I am truly blessed to be another of your creations, just as my mother is.

Carnival is the festival of freedom birthed in the twin-island republic of Trinidad and Tobago, and soca music will unite the world.

Love,
Lah Lah

Papa + Lah Lah

THIS IS A BORZOI BOOK PUBLISHED BY ALFRED A. KNOPF

Text copyright © 2024 by Nailah Blackman
Jacket art and interior illustrations copyright © 2024 by Jade Orlando

All rights reserved. Published in the United States by Alfred A. Knopf, an imprint of
Random House Children's Books, a division of Penguin Random House LLC, New York.

Knopf, Borzoi Books, and the colophon are registered trademarks of Penguin Random House LLC.

Visit us on the Web! rhcbooks.com

Educators and librarians, for a variety of teaching tools,
visit us at RHTeachersLibrarians.com

Library of Congress Cataloging-in-Publication Data
Names: Blackman-Thornhill, Nailah, author. | Orlando, Jade, illustrator.
Title: Love, Lah Lah / Nailah Blackman-Thornhill ; [illustrated by] Jade Orlando.
Description: First edition. | New York : Alfred A. Knopf, 2024. | Audience: Ages 3–7. |
Summary: "A girl and her grandpa enjoy Carnival together."—Provided by publisher.
Identifiers: LCCN 2022045624 (print) | LCCN 2022045625 (ebook) | ISBN 978-0-593-48769-3
(hardcover) | ISBN 978-0-593-48770-9 (library binding) | ISBN 978-0-593-48771-6 (ebook)
Subjects: CYAC: Stories in rhyme. | Carnival—Fiction. | Trinidadians—Fiction. | LCGFT: Stories in rhyme. |
Picture books. Classification: LCC PZ8.3.B5734 Lo 2024 (print) | LCC PZ8.3.B5734 (ebook) | DDC [E]—dc23

The text of this book is set in 18.5-point Filson Pro.
The illustrations were created using watercolors and digital tools.
Photograph of Ras Shorty I courtesy of the author.
Book design by Taline Boghosian

MANUFACTURED IN CHINA
10 9 8 7 6 5 4 3 2 1
First Edition

Random House Children's Books supports the
First Amendment and celebrates the right to read.